Dear Parent:
Your child's love of readi...

Every child learns to read in a different way and at his or her own speed. Some go back and forth between reading levels and read favorite books again and again. Others read through each level in order. You can help your young reader improve and become more confident by encouraging his or her own interests and abilities. From books your child reads with you to the first books he or she reads alone, there are I Can Read Books for every stage of reading:

SHARED READING
Basic language, word repetition, and whimsical illustrations, ideal for sharing with your emergent reader

BEGINNING READING
Short sentences, familiar words, and simple concepts for children eager to read on their own

READING WITH HELP
Engaging stories, longer sentences, and language play for developing readers

READING ALONE
Complex plots, challenging vocabulary, and high-interest topics for the independent reader

ADVANCED READING
Short paragraphs, chapters, and exciting themes for the perfect bridge to chapter books

I Can Read Books have introduced children to the joy of reading since 1957. Featuring award-winning authors and illustrators and a fabulous cast of beloved characters, I Can Read Books set the standard for beginning readers.

A lifetime of discovery begins with the magical words **"I Can Read!"**

Visit www.icanread.com for information
on enriching your child's reading experience.

Ree Drummond and Diane deGroat gratefully
acknowledge the editorial and artistic contributions
of Amanda Glickman and Rick Whipple.

I Can Read Book® is a trademark of HarperCollins Publishers.

ISBN 978-0-06-221918-3 (trade bdg.) —ISBN 978-0-06-221917-6 (pbk.)

18 19 20 SCP 10 9 8 7 ❖ First Edition

I Can Read!

BEGINNING 1 READING

CHARLIE
the Ranch Dog
CHARLIE GOES TO THE DOCTOR

based on the CHARLIE THE RANCH DOG books
by REE DRUMMOND, The Pioneer Woman
and DIANE deGROAT

HARPER
An Imprint of HarperCollinsPublishers

Something pokes my nose.

Go away!

I am so sleepy.

I peel one eyelid open.

Mama holds a juicy piece of bacon!

Sniff, sniff.

Bacon?

I can't smell it.

I can't smell anything!

My tummy feels funny.

I'm not even hungry for bacon.

What is wrong with me?

Fingers scratch my floppy ears.

Mama scoops me up and snuggles me.

I hang my head over her arm.

The driveway!

Hooray!

I love riding in the truck.

Bump. Bump. Bump.

Ouch.

Maybe I *don't* like riding in the truck.

It's like my belly is full of rocks.

When we stop, I look out the window.

What? Uh-oh.

I see the sign.

That's where the doctor lives!

RROOWW...ack...erk...croak!

Oh no. I sound like a frog.

Mama carries me inside.

I am shaking all over.

The waiting room is almost empty.

One dog looks like me, but smaller.

He has a mama, too.

She calls him Hickory.

Hickory looks scared.

I know how he feels!

$4

Dr. Jan smiles a big smile.

She doesn't fool me for one minute, though.

We go to the exam room.

Dr. Jan strokes my back.

Maybe she's not so bad.

Ahh! My eyes!

She shines a bright light into them.

I can't see!

Next, Dr. Jan scratches my ears.

Ooh, that's nice—

But then she lifts my ears up high.

That is not what floppy ears

are supposed to do!

Dr. Jan starts snooping in my mouth.

Mama says I have bad breath.

I yawn a huge yawn at Dr. Jan.

She walks away!

One can hardly blame her.

Oh no!

Dr. Jan is back.

She has big tools

in her hand.

Get those things away from me!

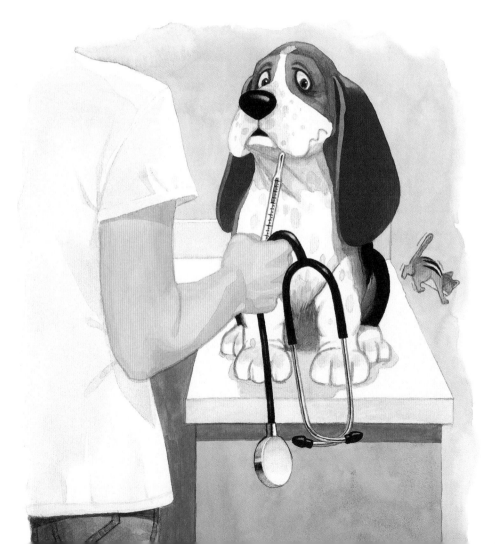

I shut my eyes tight.

I imagine I'm chasing a turtle.

Huh?

Dr. Jan is leaving again.

Boy, that was fast.

I didn't even feel anything!

We go back to the waiting room.

Dr. Jan says I'm a good boy.

She asks us to wait.

Mama's lap is cozy and warm.

Maybe it's time for a snooze.

ZZZZZZZZZZZZZ—

Huh?

Who's that under the seat?

Hickory!

Hickory whimpers.

He looks up at me.

His eyes are sad and scared.

Hickory's mama calls his name.

Dr. Jan looks behind the counter.

Hickory is hiding!

I know how Hickory feels.

I was afraid at first, too.

I smile my biggest smile

to show Hickory it won't be so bad.

It's true.

Dr. Jan did some strange things,

but she didn't hurt me one bit!

Hickory tilts his head.

I give him a sniff, sniff

and tell him not to worry.

Hickory runs to his mama.

They head to the exam room.

Hickory gives me a woof good-bye.

Bye, Hickory!

Stay in touch!

After a really, really long time,

Dr. Jan comes back.

She scratches my ears,

gives Mama a small bottle,

and says, "Charlie will be fine!"

The truck bumps all the way home.

Finally, I sprawl out on the sofa.

Mama opens the bottle from Dr. Jan.

She puts one small pill in my mouth.

It tastes like a piece of chalk.

I'd rather have a piece of bacon.

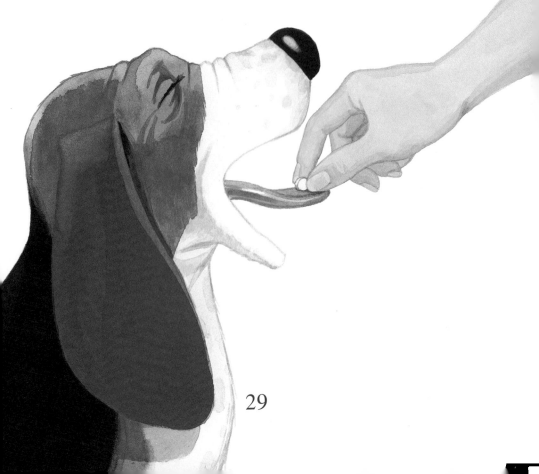

Gurgle. Grumble. Rumble.

My belly is noisy.

Hey! It's morning!

Morning means breakfast.

Sniff, sniff.

What a wonderful smell.

Oh, yummy bacon!

I sprint into the kitchen.

Mama scratches my ears while I eat.

I sniff her face.

Mama gives me a kiss on the nose.

I'm all better now!